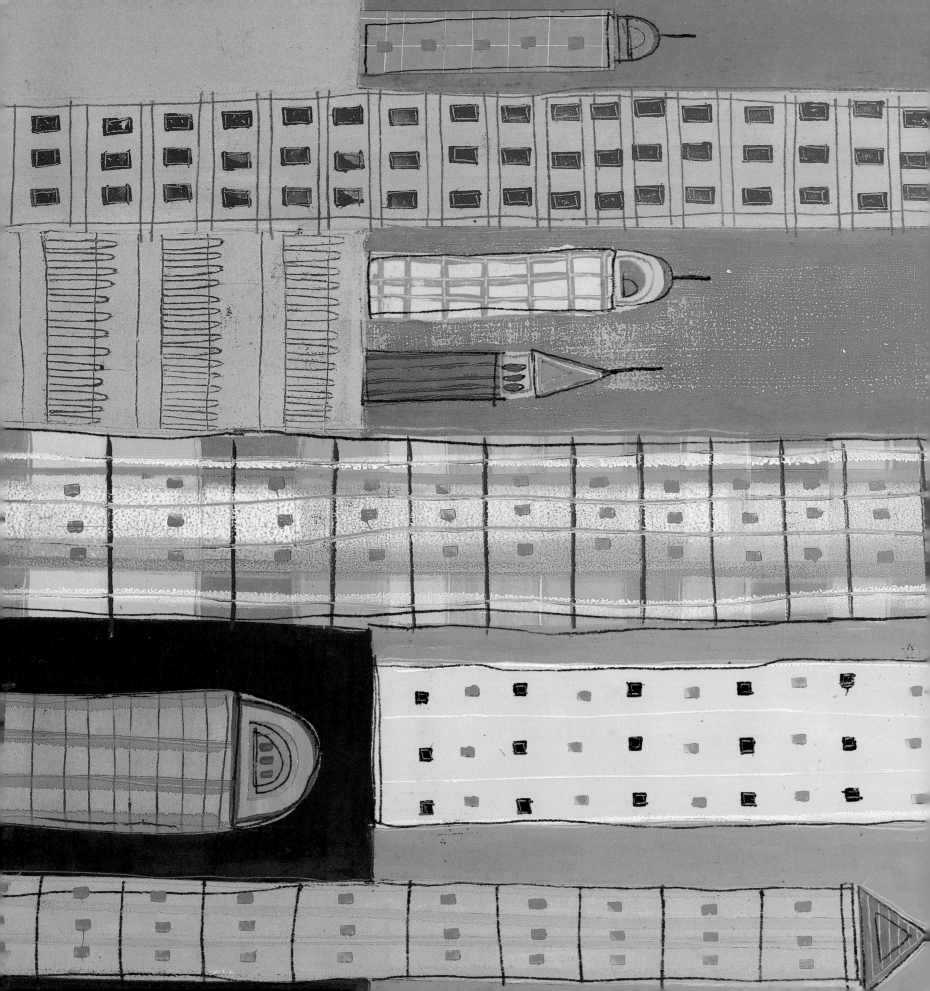

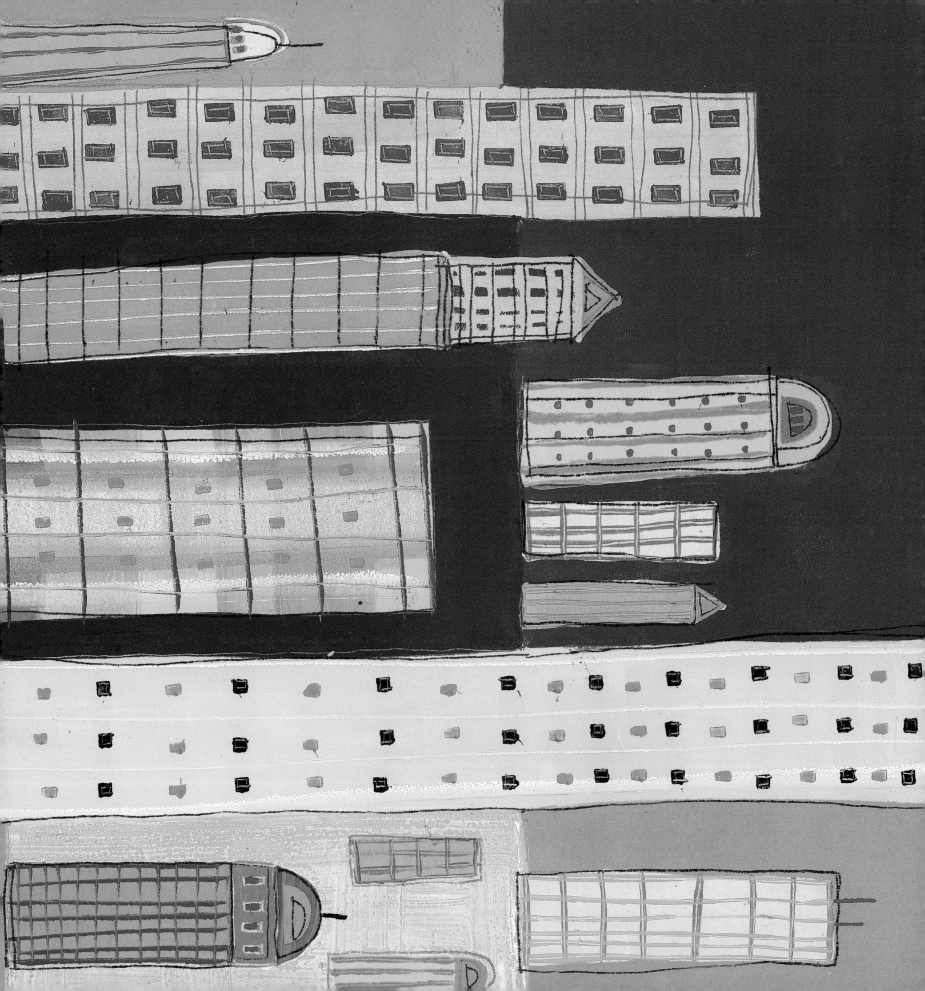

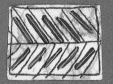
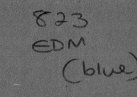

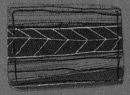

To Mum and Dad, for making me proud of who I am
L.E.

For Matthew, with love
A.W.

AN AFRICAN PRINCESS
A PICTURE CORGI BOOK 0 552 55033 7

First published in Great Britain by Doubleday,
an imprint of Random House Children's Books

Doubleday edition published 2004
Picture Corgi edition published 2005

1 3 5 7 9 10 8 6 4 2

Text copyright © Lyra Edmonds, 2004
Illustrations copyright © Anne Wilson, 2004

Picture Corgi Books are published by Random House Children's Books,
61–63 Uxbridge Road, London W5 5SA,
a division of The Random House Group Ltd,
in Australia by Random House Australia (Pty) Ltd,
20 Alfred Street, Milsons Point, Sydney, NSW 2061, Australia,
in New Zealand by Random House New Zealand Ltd,
18 Poland Road, Glenfield, Auckland 10, New Zealand,
and in South Africa by Random House (Pty) Ltd,
Endulini, 5A Jubilee Road, Parktown 2193, South Africa

THE RANDOM HOUSE GROUP Limited Reg. No. 954009
www.kidsatrandomhouse.co.uk

A CIP catalogue record for this book is available from the British Library.

Printed in Singapore

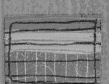

An African Princess

Lyra Edmonds

Illustrated by Anne Wilson

PICTURE CORGI

My name is Lyra and I am
an African princess.

A long time ago a princess was
captured from Africa and
taken to the Caribbean to
live. The princess had
many children, who also
had children, and soon
there were too many
princesses to count.

My mama says that we too
are part of that story, which
has spread far from Africa
to every shore.

So when I walk tall in my robe
and crown, I am a princess too.
Can you see?

At school when they poke fun and say,

"You, an African princess?
Don't be silly!"
"Where's your palace?"

I get very worried that Mama may be wrong.
There are not many African princesses who live
on the tenth floor and have freckles like me.

Mama asks where my crown and fine robe have gone.

"Maybe I'm not a princess at all," I say.

She cuddles me close and whispers, "We'll see."

One frosty day when the windows are all patterns and snakes, Mama shows me some tickets.

"We're going on holiday, to see our African Princess, Taunte May."

At school I can't wait to tell.
Standing on tiptoes I point to the place where my princess lives.

Dad and I make a calendar.

Each night I draw a cross and wish
for the days to go more quickly.

Until one day when there are no more days left.

The door opens on a
hot wet world, full of
banana trees and
humming birds. A new
sky wiggles before my
eyes and palm trees
everywhere wave their
friendly arms at me.

I feel the words bubble
up inside me and escape
my mouth.

"Hello, I'm Lyra. I'm
an African princess.
Can you see?"

On the savannah where Mama played
as a child, a man sings out loud as he
chip chops a small hole in a coconut.

"Drink fresh coconut to make you
strong like a lion."

We begin to look
for Taunte May on
a hill with a canopy of
guava and sapodilla trees.

"I hope," pants Mama,
"that I can remember
the way."

And I think I can hear the monkeys giggle and say, "We know her, she's an African princess, tee hee."

Then Mama points ahead, not at a palace, but to a little brown house on stilts.

"Mama, are you sure?" I ask, but she is already tapping on the shutters.

A soft voice calls from within.

Inside it's dark and cool.
I blink and rub my eyes.
There in front of me is an old lady.

No crown or fine robe.
Suddenly all the bubbles
inside me disappear.

Is *this* my African princess?

Then Taunte May smiles and calls me
near. She talks of princesses from long
ago and princesses around the world,
who are all part of my big family tree.

Much later, as we leave,
she whispers in my ear,
"Remember to be proud
of who you are."
And I nod and smile my
happiest princess smile.

Now when they say,
"You, an African princess?
Don't be silly!"

I walk tall and say,
"I'm Lyra,
I'm an African princess.
That's me."

 If you liked this book, you'll love . . .

Beegu

by Alexis Deacon

Jitterbug Jam

by Barbara Jean Hicks and Alexis Deacon

Willy the Wizard

by Anthony Browne

The Big Ugly Monster and the Little Stone Rabbit

by Chris Wormell

The Hoppameleon

by Paul Geraghty